Oink

For our first grandchild, with love

First American edition published 2019 by Gecko Press USA,
an imprint of Gecko Press Ltd.

First published by Gecko Press
PO Box 9335, Wellington 6141, New Zealand
info@geckopress.com

Distributed in the United States and Canada by Lerner Publishing Group, lernerbooks.com
Distributed in the United Kingdom by Bounce Sales and Marketing, bouncemarketing.co.uk
Distributed in Australia by Scholastic Australia, scholastic.com.au
Distributed in New Zealand by Upstart Distribution, upstartpress.co.nz

davidelliot.org

Gecko Press acknowledges the generous support of Creative New Zealand.

ARTS COUNCIL OF NEW ZEALAND TOI AOTEAROA

Design and typesetting by Vida and Luke Kelly Design
Printed in China by Everbest Printing Co. Ltd, an accredited ISO 14001 & FSC certified printer

MIX
Paper from
responsible sources
FSC® C124385

ISBN hardback: 978-1-776572-14-4

For more curiously good books, visit geckopress.com

Oink

David Elliot

GECKO PRESS

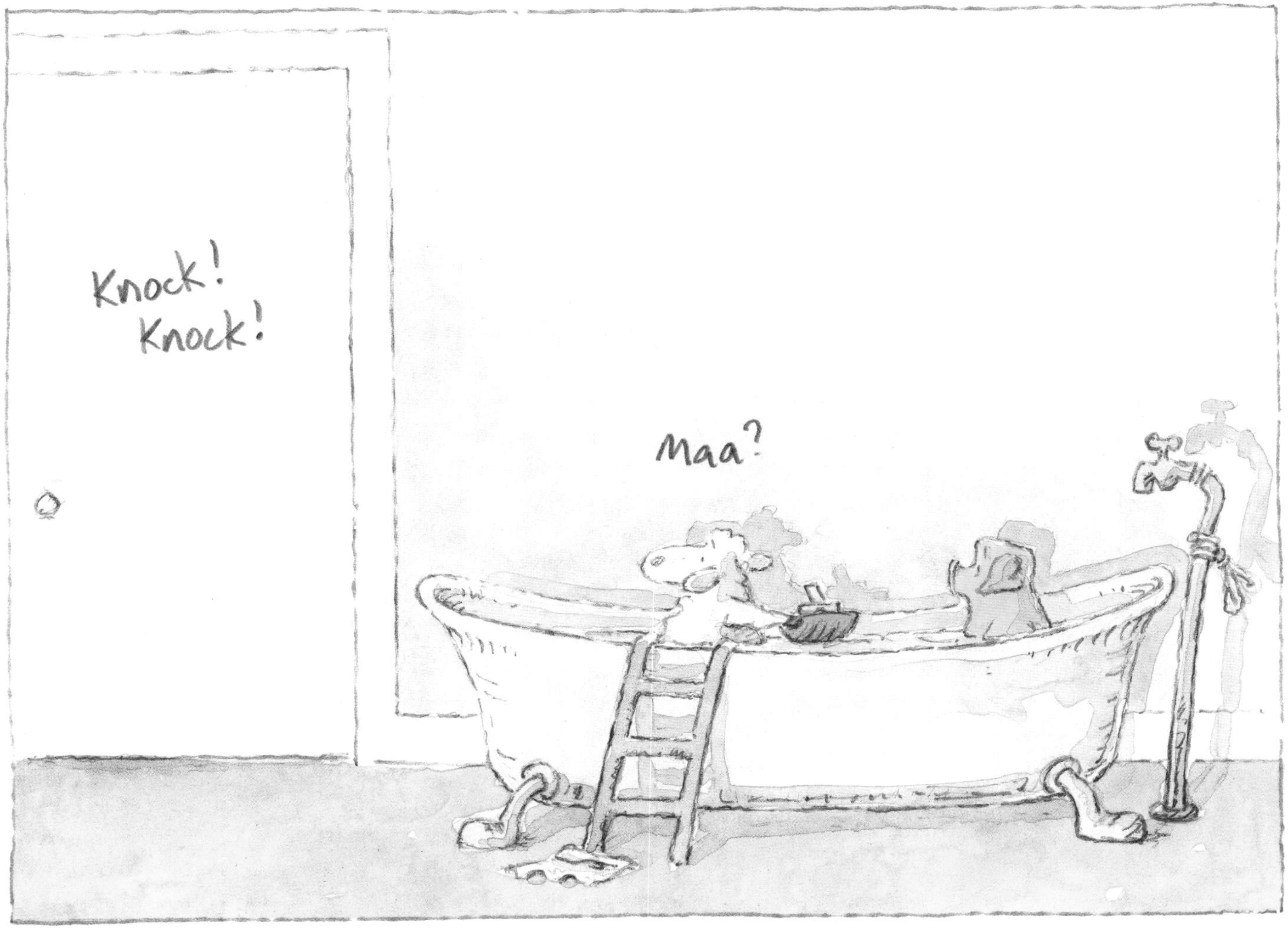
Knock!
Knock!
Maa?

Knock!
Knock!

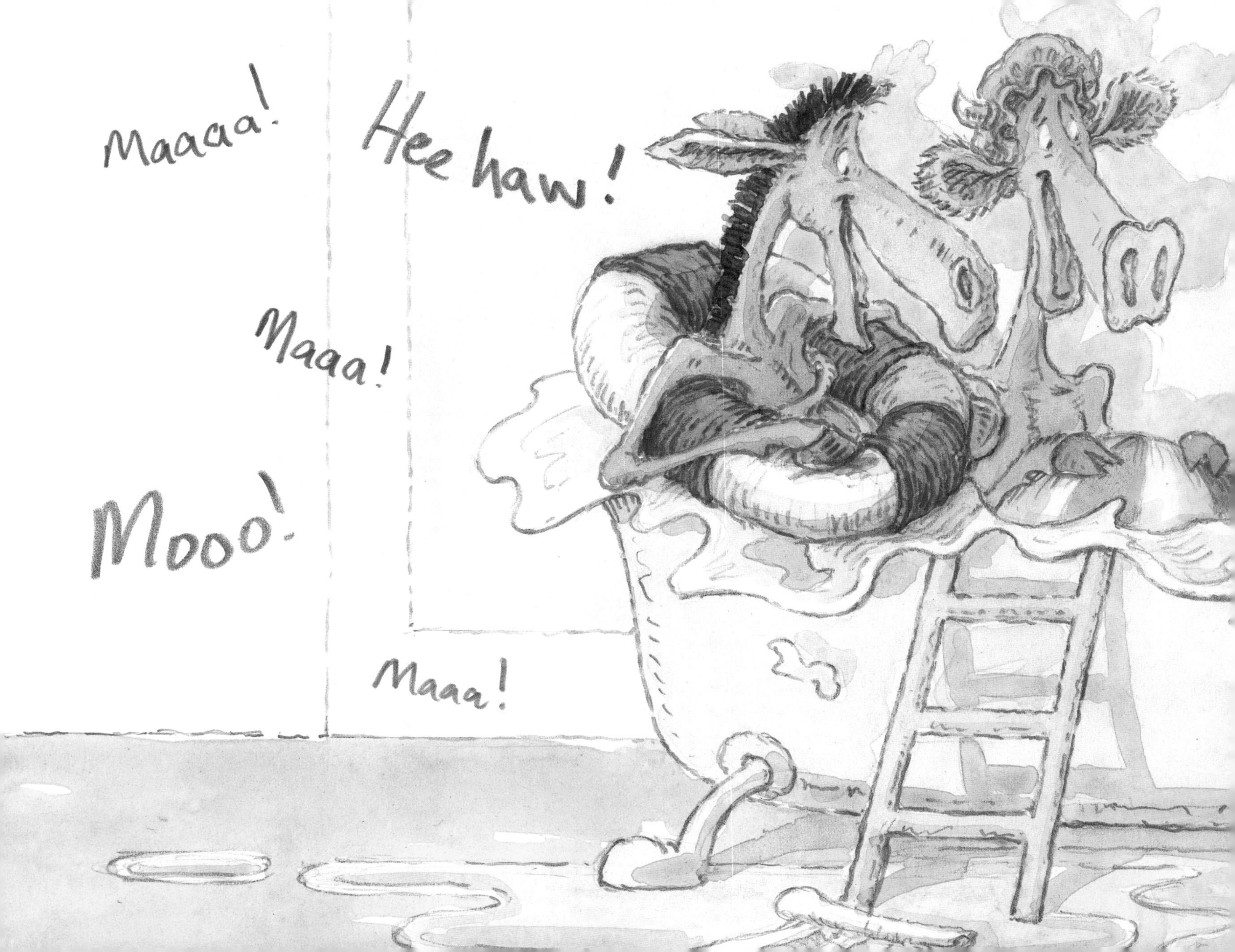
Maaaa!
Hee haw!
Maaa!
Mooo!
Maaa!

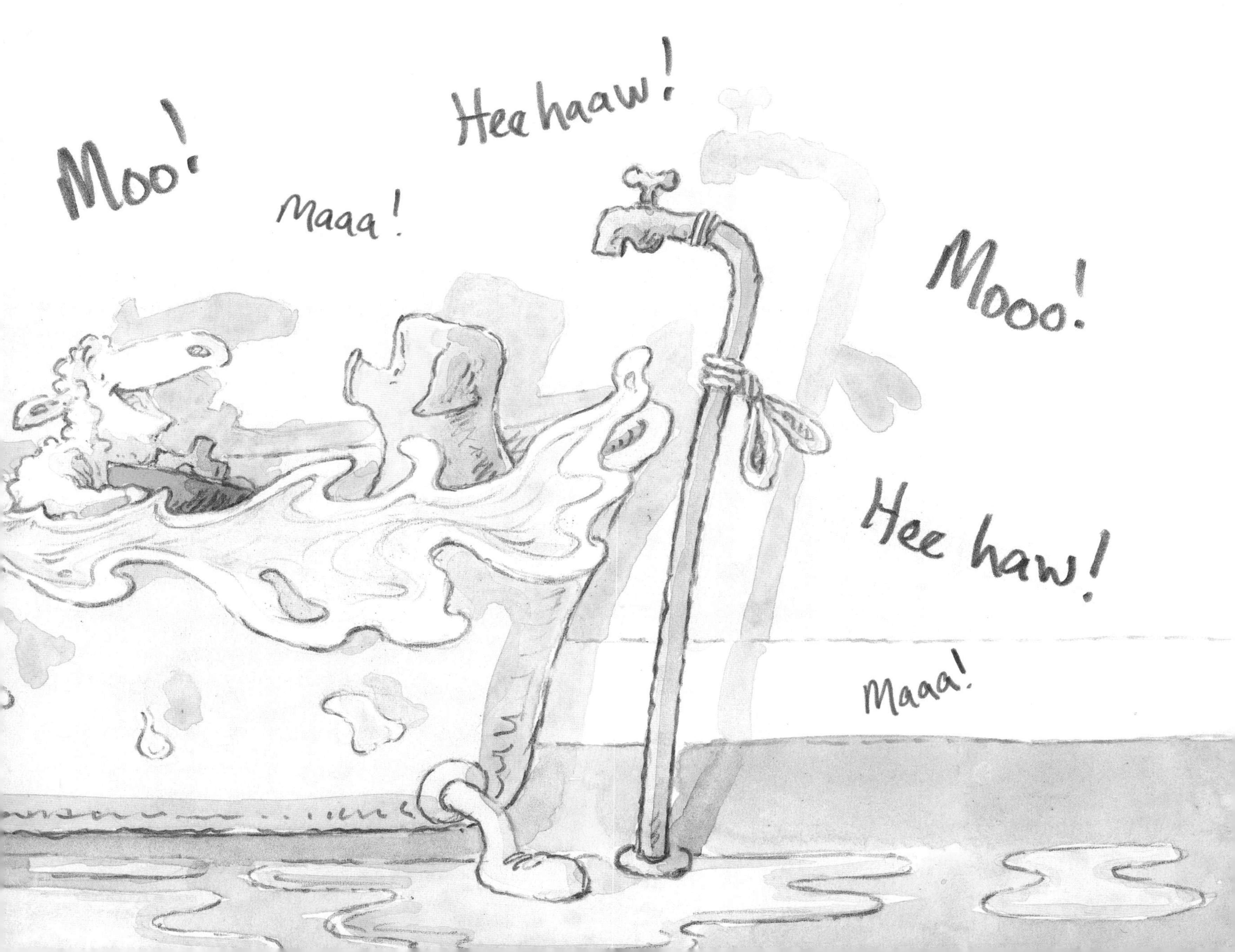
Moo!
Maaa!
Heehaaw!
Mooo!
Hee haw!
Maaa!